PENELOPE FRITTER:
SUPER-SITTER

Book#2: Meet the Phonees

BY JESSICA WOLLMAN

ILLUSTRATED BY CHRIS MACNEIL

Aladdin Paperbacks

New York London Toronto Sydney

ALADDIN PAPERBACKS
An imprint of Simon & Schuster Children's Publishing Division
1230 Avenue of the Americas, New York, NY 10020
Text copyright © 2005 by Jessica Wollman and Daniel Ehrenhaft
Illustrations copyright © 2005 by Chris MacNeil
All rights reserved, including the right of
reproduction in whole or in part in any form.
ALADDIN PAPERBACKS and colophon are
trademarks of Simon & Schuster, Inc.
Designed by Debra Sfetsios
The text of this book was set in Golden Cockerel.
Manufactured in the United States of America
First Aladdin Paperbacks edition October 2005
2 4 6 8 10 9 7 5 3 1
Library of Congress Control Number 2004118397
ISBN-13: 978-1-4169-0090-0
ISBN-10: 1-4169-0090-X

For Ernie, Beth, and Jim—because they were
not at all like Chip

Introduction

When we last left Penelope Fritter, Super-Sitter . . .

She had just used her shocking superpowers to save the world and triumph over evil.

Well, okay . . . her superpowers weren't really all that shocking. And technically, she never saved the world—just two very awful brats. Also, she hadn't exactly "triumphed," because the villain got away . . . and, to be honest, the villain—Vlad Black—wasn't so evil. He was just a crooked smoothie stand owner. And his smoothies weren't even that tasty.

But none of that is particularly important, because Penelope soon found herself embroiled in yet another amazing baby-sitting adventure—one packed with even more suspense and mayhem, not to mention frantic Jell-O eating, fiendish cakes, and freakish word scrambles.

PART I

Did Somebody Say "Chip"?

CHAPTER ONE

Penelope's Plan
to Be More Visible

Penelope Fritter was tired of being invisible.

It would be one thing if she could *choose* to be invisible—if, for instance, she could disappear whenever she wanted. But Penelope's invisibility didn't work that way. No, sadly, it boiled down to a simple problem: When people looked at Penelope, they tended to *overlook* her. If they saw her, they usually gazed right past her. If they met her, they often forgot all about her. And it wasn't because they were trying to be cruel, or trying

1

to prove a point, or they had better things to do.

Penelope simply didn't grab people's attention.

She wasn't very big, and she wasn't very small, either. She didn't dye her hair a superbright color, and she didn't have a favorite pair of clunky shoes. She didn't laugh like a clown, or shout like a sports announcer, or sneeze like an elephant.

In other words, there was nothing at all remarkable about Penelope Fritter that set her apart from other kids.

Actually, that's not quite true. Penelope did possess shocking superpowers. But she wanted to keep those a secret. Truth be told, she never wanted to use her shocking superpowers again. Luckily for her, those shocking superpowers could only be triggered by eating something strawberry. Unluckily for her, strawberry also happened to be her favorite flavor . . . but we'll get to all that later.

For now, all you need to know is that Penelope only wanted people to notice her for being her regular old self, which was perfectly nice and perfectly smart—and in spite of this somewhat lousy state of affairs, pretty wise and funny, too.

The good news was that for the first time ever, she had a plan to be more visible.

The plan involved her school, Clearwater Elementary.

Every autumn Clearwater Elementary held a school-wide celebration called Pumpkin Fest.

Incidentally, nobody could remember exactly why the celebration was called Pumpkin Fest, as it mostly involved a big turkey-sandwich-making competition. There was also a big fuss made about autumn leaves—with lots of songs and speeches about the beauty of autumn leaves and a big leaf-raking competition. But pumpkins did play a small role. For example, everybody carved up pumpkins for decorations. They also ate pumpkin pies for dessert.

In any event, such a tremendous celebration naturally required weeks and weeks of careful preparation. The teachers always asked students to volunteer to help out. This year Mr. Willard, Penelope's English teacher, was head of the Decorations Committee.

"I need volunteers to help out with decorating the gym for the upcoming Pumpkin Fest!" Mr. Willard announced during English class one day. "We need lots of carved pumpkins and lots of leaf collages! We'll meet tomorrow after school in the gym!"

Penelope thought to herself, *If I help design the most beautiful, most stunning, most extraordinary decorations in Pumpkin Fest history, people might start to remember who I am.*

After class she approached Mr. Willard.

"Um . . . hi," she said shyly.

"Yes?" Mr. Willard grumbled from behind his desk. "Can I help you?"

Penelope waited until the rest of the kids had filed out of the classroom. She tried to muster a confident smile. "Yes," she replied. "I was, um, just wondering— could I volunteer to be your assistant on the Pumpkin Fest Decorations Committee this year?"

He furrowed his bushy gray eyebrows. "And you are . . . ?"

"I'm Penelope," she said.

"I see." Mr. Willard scratched his jowly chin. "Well, I'm sorry, Philanthropy. That's very kind of you to offer. But I'm afraid you must be a student at Clearwater Elementary in order to participate in any Pumpkin Fest activities."

Penelope's shoulders sagged. "But I *am* a student here," she said quietly. "I'm a student in your class. You've taught me English for two straight years in a row."

Mr. Willard blinked at her. "What did you say your name was?"

"Penelope," she said again. Then she took a deep breath and added, "Penelope Fritter."

"Fritter?" he cried. He bolted upright, his face brightening. "As in Chip Fritter's younger sister? My goodness!

Forgive me! How could I have been so forgetful? Yes, yes, of course you can be my assistant. It would be an honor."

Penelope hung her head. "Uh … thanks," she mumbled. She slunk out the door.

"You know, it's such a shame Chip graduated," Mr. Willard called after her. "We could really use his help in this year's Pumpkin Fest. He did such a great job making the turkey sandwiches and stringing up the leaf collage banners last year. Is there anything he *can't* do?"

CHAPTER TWO

Penelope's System for Dealing with Chip

As you might have already guessed, Penelope had an older brother named Chip. And, as you also might have already guessed, Chip Fritter wasn't just *any* older brother.

Nobody ever overlooked Chip Fritter. (Not once.) Nobody ever forgot his name, either. (Or mispronounced it.) Chip Fritter could *never* disappear, even if he wanted to. (He never wanted to.) *Somebody* would always be sure to find him. And when that somebody found him, he or she would say, "Chip Fritter? I can't believe it's you! You're a real superstar!"

Unless, of course, that somebody was Penelope.

It wasn't as if Penelope didn't love Chip. Of course she did. He was her older brother. She just couldn't figure out why everybody put him in the "real superstar" category. Sure, he scored a lot of winning goals on the Clearwater High soccer team. And yes, he often helped old ladies across the street. And, okay, he *had* rescued two separate kittens from two different trees during the past year. But as far as Penelope was concerned, that was just normal nice-person-type stuff. *Anybody* could do that.

Still, Penelope had decided long ago not to worry about all the attention Chip got. In fact, she had a system for not worrying about it. Every single time anyone asked the question, "Is there anything Chip Fritter can't do?" Penelope said to herself, *I wish I had a penny for every single time people asked that question.* She'd gone so far as to create an imaginary piggy bank in her head to keep all those imaginary pennies.

Thanks to Mr. Willard, that imaginary piggy bank now held precisely $716.86.

7

CHAPTER THREE

Pumpkin Fest
Gets a New Name

After school the next day Penelope reported to the school gym to meet with Mr. Willard and the Pumpkin Fest Decorations Committee. As it turned out, lots of other students had volunteered to help out as well—more than Penelope would have expected, even. There was Fred from homeroom (who called her Priscilla), and Eve from math (who called her Prudence), and Felicia from science (who called her Pat). Most of the Clearwater Elementary teachers wanted to help out too.

The gym was packed. Even Principal Blarney was there, busily chatting away about which banners should hang where, and who should deliver which speech about the beauty of autumn leaves.

For a moment Penelope stood in the gym doorway.

She swallowed, feeling shyer than ever. She was half-tempted to turn around and go home. But then she thought, *No. I have a plan to be more visible, and I'm going to stick to it.* Besides, she had spent the previous night baking a huge batch of scrumptious homemade chocolate chip cookies. She planned to offer them as a snack to Mr. Willard and the other volunteers. She figured that if everyone on the Decorations Committee enjoyed the cookies, they would finally remember her name.

It was worth a try, at least.

Principal Blarney spotted Penelope standing by herself. "Yes, young lady?" he asked. "Can I help you?"

"Uh . . . yes," she murmured. "Hi. I'm here to help out with the decorations. I volunteered in Mr. Willard's English class."

Everyone in the gym turned toward her.

Principal Blarney raised his slim eyebrow. His forehead crinkled under his thinning hair. "And you are . . . ?"

"Penelope," she replied. As fast as she could, she

swung her knapsack off her shoulder and dug out the plastic container she'd packed full of cookies. "I brought some snacks for everyone too!"

"How nice," Principal Blarney commented.

Penelope held up the container for everyone to see. "Try one. They're homemade chocolate chip—"

Principal Blarney gasped. He looked stricken.

"What's the matter?" Penelope asked.

"Did you say Chip?" Principal Blarney asked. "Chip—as in, Chip Fritter?"

"Uh . . ." Penelope wasn't sure how to respond.

"Chip *Fritter?*" several people cried in the silence.

"Boy, we could really use him for the Decorations Committee!" Fred from Penelope's homeroom exclaimed.

"He did such a great job last year!" Mr. Willard added.

"That boy's a real superstar!" shouted Felicia from science.

"Hear, hear," Principal Blarney agreed. "Is there anything Chip Fritter *can't* do?"

Before Penelope even had time to add another penny to her imaginary piggy bank, the entire crowd was buzzing with talk of Chip. *Hmm.* Her lips turned downward. Maybe baking chocolate chip cookies *wasn't* such a great idea. She should have baked peanut butter or oatmeal cookies. Anything without chips . . .

Just then Principal Blarney let out a piercing whistle: "PHHHEW-EET!"

"People, I have a great idea," he proclaimed.

A hush fell over the crowd.

"This year, in honor of the boy we love so dearly, I propose we rename Pumpkin Fest," Principal Blarney said. "I propose we call it 'Chip Fritter Fest.' All those in favor, raise your hands."

Every single person in the gym threw a hand into the air.

Every single person, that is, except Penelope.

CHAPTER FOUR

The Rest of Penelope's Miserable Afternoon

Have you ever heard the old saying: "Things went downhill from there"?

Maybe you have. Maybe you've even pictured something—or maybe even some*one*—rolling downhill, tumbling faster and faster, getting dirtier and dirtier, and finally splashing into a filthy puddle at the bottom of a steep slope. If you've pictured that, then you have a pretty good idea of what the rest of Penelope's afternoon was like.

To be honest, Penelope would have *preferred* to be lying in the middle of a filthy puddle. She would have preferred that to what actually happened, which went as follows:

For starters, the entire Pumpkin Fest Decorations Committee tossed out all their old Pumpkin Fest banners, streamers, and posters. As soon as they had mashed them into the garbage, they got straight to work on creating a batch of brand-new banners, streamers, and posters. Every single one featured a portrait of Chip.

They also gobbled down all of Penelope's scrumptious homemade chocolate chip cookies while they worked. Unfortunately, Penelope had written her first and last name on the cookie tin, so the group quickly learned she was Chip Fritter's sister. But, of course, they *still* couldn't remember her name.

"Great cookies, Parker!" said Principal Blarney. "Did Chip give you the recipe?"

"These really are good," said Fred from homeroom, his mouth full of crumbs. "They remind me of those pumpkin pies Chip baked for Pumpkin Fest last year."

"Pat, what's it like to live with the Chipster?" asked Felicia from science.

When Penelope finally shambled out of the gym to

go home, her imaginary piggy bank held $717.04 in imaginary pennies. But that wasn't even the most depressing part. The most depressing part was imagining how many pennies her piggy bank would hold after the big Chip Fritter Fest.

CHAPTER FIVE

The Big "Chip Fritter Fest"

In the old days Clearwater Elementary always held Pumpkin Fest on a Thursday morning. But seeing as the entire celebration had been completely changed and renamed in honor of Chip, Principal Blarney decided to hold Chip Fritter Fest on a Thursday *evening*. That way, every single person in Clearwater, young or old, could attend. They wouldn't have to miss school or work, either. Principal Blarney figured *everyone* would want a chance to spend time with the Chipster.

"You know, I think it was really nice of Principal

Blarney to move Chip Fritter Fest to a Thursday night," Chip stated on the drive over to school. "Before, only kids at school were able to spend time with me. Now everybody gets a chance."

"I agree," said Mom cheerily.

"Hear, hear," said Dad from behind the wheel. "Nobody wants to miss another Chip Fritter Fest."

"But this is the *first* Chip Fritter Fest," Penelope mumbled from the backseat. "It wasn't even *called* Chip Fritter Fest before. It was called *Pumpkin* Fest."

"What was that, sweetie?" Mom asked.

"Never mind," groaned Penelope.

Chip patted Penelope's knee. "Don't worry," he said. "You'll get to spend some time with the Chipster at this year's Chip Fritter Fest too."

CHAPTER SIX

Penelope Plans to Spend as Little Time as Possible with the Chipster

At least Clearwater Elementary hadn't entirely abandoned the old Pumpkin Fest. Sure, there were plenty of posters and banners of Chip hanging all over the gym. But the first annual Chip Fritter Fest wasn't *only* about Chip. Penelope was very relieved to discover the same old turkey-sandwich-making competition inside, and the same old leaf-raking competition outside—and she spotted Principal Blarney himself standing behind a huge table full of pumpkins at the back of the gym, just as he always had.

The moment the Fritter family appeared, Principal Blarney let out one of his signature whistles: "PHHHEW-EET!"

"I'd like to thank you all for coming to the first annual Chip Fritter Fest!" he announced. "It looks to me like the entire town showed up!"

Penelope had to agree. The gym was so crowded that she could hardly move.

"And who better to kick off the celebration than the Chipster himself?" Principal Blarney continued. "So please, let's give a warm Clearwater Elementary welcome to the one, the only, a real superstar . . . CHIP FRITTER!!!"

The gym erupted in feverish applause.

There were hoots and hollers. People clapped and stamped their feet. Some even chanted: "CHIP-STER . . . CHIP-STER . . . CHIP-STER . . ."

Everybody made a huge racket.

Everybody, that is, except Penelope.

As Chip made his way through the crowd toward Principal Blarney—shaking hands with adoring fans as he went—Penelope squirmed her way back toward the front doors.

She wasn't upset. Honestly. She simply wanted some space to breathe.

Well . . . that, and she'd also made another decision. Another plan, really. She intended to stick to it too, just as she'd stuck to her plan of volunteering for the Pumpkin Fest Decorations Committee last week.

Her new plan was: *I am going to spend as little time with Chip as possible tonight.*

When Chip finally reached the pumpkin table, the chanting began to die down.

"Thanks so much, people of Clearwater!" he cried. "Hey, I've got a fantastic idea! Let's have a pumpkin-carving competition this year too! Whoever carves the best, coolest, pumpkin ever gets to come over to my house and hang out with me! They also get to eat my sister's delicious chocolate chip cookies!"

Everybody cheered. Everybody except you-know-who.

"That *is* a fantastic idea," Principal Blarney agreed. "But why leave it at that? I say we turn this new pumpkin-carving competition into a Chip-Fritter-carving competition. Whoever carves a pumpkin that looks most like the Chipster wins!"

"Hear, hear!" the people shouted. Everybody descended on the pumpkins immediately. It reminded Penelope of an elephant stampede. Her own parents eagerly rushed to the front of the herd.

Penelope, however, remained by the doorway. In a matter of moments she was all alone. And right then, she came up with yet another new plan.

I'm going to go home, she decided. *That way, I'll have the whole house to myself. I can finish my homework, or do word scrambles—or even bake homemade cookies, just for me, and definitely* not *chocolate chip. Besides, if I leave now, that's one less person who will be participating in the pumpkin-carving competition. So everybody else will have a better chance at winning. So I'm really* not *doing this for* me. *I'm doing this for* them. *And, of course, for Chip. Tonight is Chip Fritter Fest. . . .*

With that, she turned and bolted out the door.

CHAPTER SEVEN

A Very Peculiar Family

Penelope didn't get very far.

In fact, she didn't get anywhere at all.

Four very tall grown-ups stood in the hallway just outside the gym, blocking her path—two tall men and two tall women. All four had gray hair.

At first Penelope intended to run right past them. But then she began to stare.

As rude as she knew staring to be, she couldn't stop herself. There was just something very, well . . . *peculiar* about this bunch. One of the men was dressed just like

Penelope's dad, in a suit. One of the women held a massively oversized handbag. And the other two grown-ups were dressed like children. The man wore striped shorts and a T-shirt, and a little cap with a plastic propeller on top. The woman wore pigtails and striped overalls, and she clutched a stuffed bear.

"Where are you going, dear?" the woman with the huge handbag asked. Her voice was surprisingly deep.

"Uh . . . me?" Penelope asked.

The woman threw her head back and laughed. The sound was loud and grating, like tires screeching on a wet road. "Yes, *you*!" she cried. "Don't you want to stay for Chip Fritter Fest?"

Penelope bit her lip. She wasn't sure if she wanted to answer that question.

"What's your name, dear?" the woman asked.

"Penelope."

"What a pretty name," the woman remarked. "Well, Penelope, we're new to town. We just moved here last week. It's sort of a funny story. We bought a lovely house. The previous owner abandoned it under mysterious circumstances." She tapped a long red-painted fingernail against her teeth. "Someone who might have gotten into trouble with the law . . . a crooked smoothie stand owner, if memory serves me correctly. I can't

remember the name. . . ." Her voice trailed off. She arched an eyebrow.

"Vlad Black?" Penelope guessed.

The woman smiled. "Yes! Precisely! Do you know him?"

Penelope shifted on her feet. She gulped anxiously. She began to wish she *had* just run right past them. "Sort of," she admitted.

"Darling, you're making Penelope uncomfortable," the man in the suit quickly piped up. "We don't need to discuss Vlad Black." He stepped forward. "Allow us to introduce ourselves. We're the Phonee Family. P-H-O-N-E-E. My name is Mr. Phonee, and this is Mrs. Phonee. And these are our darling children, Boris and Ophelia

Phonee." He gestured toward the gray-haired man in the propeller cap and the gray-haired woman with the stuffed animal.

"Nice to meet you, Penelope," Boris said.

"Yes, very nice!" cried Ophelia. She laughed the same terrible laugh as her mother.

Penelope tried not to wince.

"How old are you, Penelope?" Boris asked.

"Twelve," Penelope replied.

Boris's eyes lit up. "I'm nine!" he yelled. "I'll be twelve in three years!"

"I'll be twelve in five years, Penelope!" Ophelia added. "I'm seven!"

Penelope glanced from one to the other. She couldn't quite bring herself to believe that Boris was nine and Ophelia was seven. What seven-year-old had gray hair? But in spite of that, and in spite of the fact that this was certainly the oddest family she had ever met in her life, Penelope couldn't help but smile—for a very simple reason.

All four Phonees had remembered her name.

CHAPTER EIGHT

Maybe Not So
Peculiar After All

"PENELOPE!" Chip's voice boomed from the back of the gym. "Where are you going? Don't you want to join the pumpkin-carving competition?"

Penelope glanced over her shoulder.

What a time to stop being invisible.

Every single person in the gym stared disapprovingly at her through the open doors. They looked as if they were silently demanding, *What sort of person leaves Chip Fritter*

Fest? Every single person was also holding a pumpkin. So Penelope felt a hundred pairs of disapproving eyes on her . . . a hundred pairs of eyes, and a hundred faceless pumpkins. It was sort of creepy—creepy in a Halloween-horror-movie-type way.

"Um, I was just making some new friends," Penelope stammered. "Chip, I'd like you to meet the Phonees. They're new in town."

"Well, why didn't you say so!" exclaimed Chip. He dashed out from behind the table and hurried through the crowd. "Welcome, welcome! I'm Chip Fritter!"

Mr. Phonee gave Chip a hearty handshake. "We know who you are, Chip," he said. "We've heard all about you."

"Oh yes," gushed Mrs. Phonee. "We've seen you in the paper and on the local news. You're a real superstar around these parts!"

"We've all asked ourselves the same question," Boris said bashfully. He stared at his feet and fiddled with the plastic propeller on his cap.

"What question is that?" asked Chip.

"Is there anything Chip Fritter *can't* do?" Ophelia squealed, giggling and squeezing her teddy bear.

Everybody burst into laughter.

Chip shrugged and smiled. Then he laughed too.

Penelope rolled her eyes. *Maybe the Phonees aren't so peculiar after all,* she grumbled to herself as she raised the imaginary piggy bank's total up to $717.05. *They're madly in love with my brother. They'll fit right in.*

CHAPTER NINE

A Town-Warming Gift

Mrs. Phonee removed a large Tupperware container from her enormous handbag and presented it to Chip. "We decided to bring a little housewarming gift to the celebration," she stated, snapping off the lid with a flourish. "Or maybe not so much a housewarming gift as a town-warming gift!" She chuckled bashfully. "We knew everybody in town would be here, so we brought our family favorite."

Penelope peered into the container. Glistening and

quivering there, smack in the middle, was a funky orange Jell-O mold shaped like a turkey.

"The secret recipe has been in our family for ages," Mrs. Phonee added, her deep voice rumbling. "Not to boast, but we're experts at making dessert. . . ."

Wait a second, Penelope thought. Suddenly, something about Mrs. Phonee's voice struck a familiar chord. *Where have I heard it before?* Penelope wondered, racking her brain. She couldn't place it, though. Maybe her imagination was getting the best of her. And as the crowd gathered around the strange turkey-shaped Jell-O mold, she shook her head. She *couldn't* have heard Mrs. Phonee's voice before. No, because she knew she definitely hadn't seen Mrs. Phonee before today. She would have remembered *that.*

"Ohh," went some of the crowd.

"Ahh," went others.

"Wow," said Chip. "That's the most incredible Jell-O mold I've ever seen!"

"Hear, hear!" everyone agreed at once.

Mr. Phonee beamed. "Why, thank you, Chip. I can't tell you how much that compliment means to me, especially coming from *you*! Would you like the first bite?"

"Oh, *please,*" Penelope muttered under her breath.

"What was that, dear?" Mrs. Phonee asked.

"Um, nothing." Penelope forced another smile. It was harder this time. She was growing grumpier by the second. "I was just wondering: Could I try a bite too, please?"

"Of course, dear," Mrs. Phonee replied, with that awful shrieking laugh. "There's plenty of Jell-O Turkey for everyone! Everyone gets a taste!" She winked at Penelope. "I know how you kids *love* dessert."

"But not as much as we love Chip Fritter!" Ophelia and Boris chimed in.

"Hear, hear!" everyone agreed again, for what seemed like the billionth time.

"Aw, thanks, folks," Chip said. "I appreciate it."

At that moment Penelope came very close to stomping out of the school with a very large scowl on her face. It was one thing to have everyone fawning over Chip all the time. And it was one thing to rename Pumpkin Fest—a fest that had absolutely *nothing* to do with Chip, Penelope might add—in Chip's honor. Penelope could handle all that. But comparing Chip to dessert? Comparing him to something so sweet and so delectable? No. That was too much. That was *wrong*.

Fortunately, before Penelope could say anything she

might regret, Mrs. Phonee handed her a large glistening, quivering bite of Jell-O Turkey. Penelope shoved the whole thing in her mouth all at once.

And she had to admit, as she chewed and savored that orange flavoring: It was the sweetest, most delectable Jell-O she had ever tasted.

CHAPTER TEN

That Feeling You Get When You Accidentally Doze Off in Class

Right after that—

Something very *weird* happened. It's a little difficult to explain, in fact.

Think of it this way: Have you ever accidentally dozed off in class? Or when you're watching TV? Have you ever been paying attention one second, then closed your eyes the next, and then jerked awake several minutes later? If you have, you know the feeling: It's that uncomfortable, strange, disoriented feeling you get when you've missed a thing or two. The problem is, you don't know *what* you missed. There's a big blank in your memory.

That's exactly how Penelope felt.

One moment she was slurping down the Phonees' delicious orange turkey Jell-O mold . . . and the very next (or so it seemed to her), she was back in her car, heading home with Chip and her parents.

"What happened?" Penelope asked groggily.

"What do you mean, sweetie?" answered Dad from behind the wheel.

Penelope blinked. She felt very confused. "Weren't we just at school, you know, celebrating Pumpkin Fest—I mean, Chip Fritter Fest?"

"Of course, dear," said Mom.

Penelope shook her head. "So . . ."

"Personally, I think this was the best Chip Fritter Fest ever," Chip said.

"But . . ." Penelope rubbed her eyes. "What happened after the Phonees passed around their orange turkey-shaped Jell-O mold?"

Nobody said a word.

Finally Dad cleared his throat. "What do you mean,

sweetie?" he asked for the second time.

"I mean, was there a pumpkin-carving competition?" she asked.

"Of course there was!" Mom, Dad, and Chip exclaimed at once.

"Well, okay," Penelope said cautiously. "Then let me put it this way: Do you *remember* the pumpkin-carving competition?"

Once again there was silence.

"Um, now that you mention it . . ." Dad began, narrowing his eyes.

"Funny you should ask that, because . . ." Mom added, gazing off into the distance.

"Well I don't remember it *exactly*," Chip cut in. "But I know there *was* a Chip Fritter Pumpkin-Carving Competition, because I won first prize. See?" He reached into his pocket and dug out a medal. "I carved the pumpkin that looked most like me! What do you guys think of it?"

Dad flashed Chip a proud grin in the rearview mirror. "Well done, Chipster."

Mom sighed happily. "I've said it before, and I'll say it again, Chip. Is there anything you *can't* do?"

Now, normally Penelope would have added another

imaginary penny to her imaginary piggy bank. But she was too baffled and bewildered. The imaginary piggy bank didn't even occur to her. (In case *you're* keeping count, though, Mrs. Fritter just pushed the total up to $717.06.) Her mind kept spinning with questions. Why couldn't she remember the pumpkin-carving competition? Or for that matter, why couldn't she remember the turkey-sandwich-making competition, or the leaf-raking competition? Why couldn't she remember *anything* about Chip Fritter Fest?

But for some reason, the question that bothered her most of all—the question she finally asked—was: "Doesn't anyone else think that the Phonees were just a little bit . . . *weird?*"

Dad shrugged. So did Mom.

"I don't think they were weird," Chip said. "They seemed to fit right in, didn't they? I mean, they'd heard all about me!"

"Of course they'd heard all about you, dear," Mom crooned.

"Who hasn't heard of the Chipster?" Dad asked.

"Nobody!" the three of them shouted together.

Everybody in the car chuckled long and hard after that.

Well, not quite everybody. Penelope remained silent.

She stared out the window, grumpily pursing her lips and folding her arms across her chest.

But, in a funny way (and not "ha-ha" funny), she was almost grateful for her strange and sudden memory problem. Because if it meant forgetting about the first annual Chip Fritter Fest, a bizarre gap in her memory really didn't seem so bad at all.

PART II

The Plot Thickens

CHAPTER ELEVEN

A Shock at
the Breakfast Table

When Penelope awoke the next morning, she felt a little guilty.

Or maybe not so much guilty as ashamed. Or maybe not so much of either. Maybe just a little of both. (A very little.) In any case, she knew she shouldn't hold a grudge against Chip. If people wanted to fawn and fuss over him, they were welcome to do so. They'd been doing it for as long as she could remember. And they would probably continue to do so for the next hundred years, or million years, or even *zillion* years . . . when everybody would be living in remote space pods near Pluto—except that Pluto would be renamed "Chip-O."

The point was, Penelope was done being angry. D-O-N-E *done*.

People could fawn and fuss over Chip all they wanted. He *was* a great guy. Maybe not a "real superstar," but . . . Whatever. She wouldn't allow it to bother her anymore. She also realized something important: If she wanted to be less invisible, she had to come up with a new plan. And maybe she could even ask Chip to help her out. Yes! After all, who better to help out with becoming more visible than the most visible kid in all Clearwater—and maybe even the entire country, and maybe even the universe?

So by the time Penelope marched down the stairs for breakfast, dressed and ready for school, she actually felt pretty good. She definitely felt better than she had yesterday. The delicious aroma of Dad's pancakes wafted all around her. *Mmm.* Her mouth began to water. If there was anything Penelope loved, it was her father's pancakes. She bounded into the kitchen. Today she was going to stuff her face with as many—

She skidded to a stop.

Her lips curled into a frown.

Something wasn't quite right in the Fritter kitchen.

No, something was definitely *wrong*.

Chip wasn't there, for one thing. Usually he made it to the table well before Penelope. But not only was he not there this morning, his seat was also occupied ... by Mrs. Phonee.

Yes, the same Mrs. Phonee whom Penelope had met last night. The same Mrs. Phonee who had passed around the strange but tasty orange turkey-shaped Jell-O mold. The same Mrs. Phonee who carried that enormous handbag, which stood on the floor next to her chair, practically as tall as the chair itself ... the same Mrs. Phonee who had struck Penelope as extremely *weird*—as did the rest of the Phonee family.

Mom sat beside Mrs. Phonee, sipping coffee. The pancakes sat in a neat stack on a tray in the middle of the table, untouched. Neither Chip nor Dad was anywhere to be seen.

"Well, hello, Penelope!" Mrs. Phonee exclaimed in that oddly familiar, deep voice of hers. "Your mother and I were just talking about you!"

Penelope drew her head back. "Really?" she asked in shock.

She wasn't shocked because Chip and her dad were nowhere to be seen, or that a relatively perfect stranger (a *weird* perfect stranger, no less) was sitting in Chip's seat.

She wasn't even shocked that Mom seemed perfectly content, as if every breakfast began with sipping coffee alongside Mrs. Phonee, who had taken Chip's seat.

Penelope was shocked because, once again, Mrs. Phonee remembered her name.

But that wasn't the most shocking thing of all.

No, the most shocking thing of all was—and Penelope honestly couldn't remember a single time this had ever happened, *ever* . . .

The most shocking thing of all was that her mom and this odd stranger had *not* been talking about Chip.

They'd been talking about *her.*

And even Penelope had to admit: That wasn't just shocking. It was downright suspicious.

CHAPTER TWELVE

Mrs. Phonee Makes the Most Awful Offer Ever

"So, anyway, Penelope," Mrs. Phonee continued, turning toward her. "I was just discussing a little offer with your mother."

Penelope stared at Mrs. Phonee. Once again, Penelope couldn't *stop* herself from staring, even though she knew it was rude. And it wasn't because she was suspicious of Mrs. Phonee—although she *was* suspicious, though she couldn't quite figure out why, aside from the fact that Mrs. Phonee remembered her name.

No, she stared because Mrs. Phonee was wearing an ill-fitting sweatshirt: a sweatshirt that prominently featured an advertisement for Vlad Black's former Smoothie Stand.

"What's the matter, dear?" Mrs. Phonee asked.

"Um ... your sweatshirt," Penelope said. "Isn't that ...?" She wanted to say, *Isn't that Vlad Black? The crooked Smoothie Stand owner? The one who tried to break into the Sips' house to steal their top secret Smoothie recipe the night that I baby-sat the Sips' two very awful brats?* But she couldn't quite bring herself to form all those words.

Mrs. Phonee burst into her horrid high-pitched laugh.

"You don't miss a thing, do you, Penelope?" she exclaimed. "Well, as I told you, we bought Vlad Black's old house. And we found a whole box of these in the garage! He must have left them behind when he fled under mysterious circumstances. And Mr. Phonee and I always say, Waste not, want not! These sweatshirts fit every member of our family perfectly. Why, Boris and Ophelia insist on wearing them all the time. They've become our favorites!"

Penelope mustered an anxious smile. Mrs. Phonee's sweatshirt didn't look like it fit perfectly. It looked as if she were wearing a small tent, or a large garbage bag.

"Anyway, Mr. Phonee and I want to go out for lunch

tomorrow," Mrs. Phonee prattled on. She sipped her coffee, her red-painted nails clicking against the mug. "You know, solo, without the kiddies. And your mother told me that you *love* to baby-sit. So I thought you might enjoy watching Boris and Ophelia while we're out. And even though they didn't get a chance to spend so much time with *you* yesterday, they just *adore* your brother. But then, who doesn't love the Chipster? What do you say?"

Penelope glanced at Mom.

She was hoping Mom would pipe up on her behalf. She was hoping Mom would proclaim, *Penelope hates to baby-sit! The last time she baby-sat she got embroiled in a wacky adventure! Not that I know anything about it, as Penelope kept it a secret from me. So I don't know anything about her shocking superpowers, either—but still! Penelope doesn't want to baby-sit your weird, overgrown, gray-haired kids! And by the way, if you really love the Chipster, shouldn't you be wondering where he is? Shouldn't you be wondering where Penelope's dad is too?*

But Mom didn't say a word.

In fact, even though Mom was sipping coffee—which Penelope knew was supposed to wake you up—she looked half-asleep.

Now that Penelope really thought about it, Mom

hadn't uttered a single word at all since Penelope had walked into the kitchen.

"So it's settled then," Mrs. Phonee concluded. "Your mother will drop you off at our new home at eleven a.m. sharp. Thanks so much, dear!"

CHAPTER THIRTEEN

A Piece of Cake

Penelope finally managed to snap out of her shocked stupor. "Um, I'm not so sure that's a good idea," she protested.

Mrs. Phonee frowned. "Why not?"

"Well, for one thing, I've got lots of homework to do this weekend," Penelope replied.

It was true. Penelope had a math test *and* an English paper due on Monday. Of course, that wasn't the reason why she thought baby-sitting the Phonee kids was such a bad idea. It was just the most polite excuse she could come up with.

"Homework!" Mrs. Phonee echoed with a chuckle. "You're such a responsible young lady. I like that in a baby-sitter. But don't worry. We'll have you home by two o'clock at the very latest. And the children always take a nice, long nap every afternoon, so you'll be able to work while they're sleeping."

Penelope chewed her lip.

"What's the matter?" Mrs. Phonee demanded. "You look like something's troubling you." She sighed and put her coffee mug down. "Oh, I know what it is. I am so sorry, Penelope—am I making you feel awkward? You wanted to ask me about money, didn't you? Well, I'll pay you five dollars an hour. How's that?"

Penelope started shaking her head. "No, no, no . . ."

Mrs. Phonee grimaced. "Well, okay. Six-fifty an hour?"

"No, I mean the money is fine," Penelope answered, blushing. "I don't even really care about getting paid—"

"So five, then," Mrs. Phonee interrupted.

"No, it's not that. I just don't think I should do it, Mrs. Phonee. I'd just feel funny about it. I don't know your kids at all. And besides . . . they're much *bigger* than I am."

Penelope tried to appear as apologetic as possible. She knew she couldn't say out loud what she was really thinking, which was that she was *frightened* of Boris and Ophelia. Not only were they much bigger than she was, but they also looked a lot older than she did—and maybe even older than Mrs. Phonee. How could she possibly get them to take a nap? How could she read them a bedtime story? What if they didn't like it?

"Oh, they're just angels," crooned Mrs. Phonee. "You'll all have a wonderful time. I promise. It'll be a piece of cake!"

Once again Penelope turned to Mom for some support, some help, *anything*. But Mom wasn't paying attention. She wasn't even sitting up straight. Worse than that, it seemed as though she'd decided to take a nap. Her head was nestled in the crook of her arm on the kitchen table, and she'd closed her eyes, snoozing beside her coffee mug with a contented grin on her face.

"Oh, and speaking of cake, that reminds me!" Mrs. Phonee cried. She bent down and reached into her enormous handbag, yanking out yet another Tupperware container and placing it on the table. "I have some coffee cake for you all as a thank-you. . . ."

Penelope's eyes narrowed suspiciously, for what seemed like the thousandth time.

There was a note taped to the top of the container. It read:

HELLO, I AM A DELICIOUS COFFEE CAKE. I TASTE BEST WHEN EATEN AT TWELVE NOON ON

SATURDAY. YOU GOT THAT? TWELVE O'CLOCK ON THE NOSE! NOT A SECOND BEFORE, AND NOT A SECOND AFTER! ☺

Penelope swallowed.

Even with the smiley face, Mrs. Phonee's cake didn't look so much like a thank-you. It looked more like a threat.

CHAPTER FOURTEEN

Cakes Don't Just Deliver
Themselves, You Know

Suddenly Mom bolted up in her chair.

"Wha—wha—what's going on?" she croaked sleepily.

"Why, nothing!" cried Mrs. Phonee, laughing. "I was just talking with your lovely daughter. She has very generously agreed to baby-sit Boris and Ophelia tomorrow."

"No, I haven't," Penelope said.

"How sweet of you, Penelope!" Mom exclaimed, taking a big swig of coffee.

Penelope pursed her lips. "But I didn't agree to—"

"Mrs. Fritter, I informed Penelope that you would drop her off at eleven a.m. and pick her up no later than two p.m.," Mrs. Phonee announced, silencing Penelope in midsentence.

Penelope felt a sinking sensation in her gut. "But that's not even what you said—"

"And now I really must get going," Mrs. Phonee interrupted once more, scooping her gigantic handbag off the floor. "I hope you enjoy your coffee cake! It's another special family recipe. I'm passing them out all around town!"

Mom smiled at Mrs. Phonee. "Would you like a piece for the road?" she asked.

"Oh, no thank you," replied Mrs. Phonee. "It's not meant for breakfast. It *has* to be eaten at lunch." She pointed to the note. "And as you can see, it tastes best when it's eaten on Saturday at noon on the nose. *On the nose,*" she repeated forcefully.

"On the nose," Mom repeated too.

Penelope glared at her. Mom didn't even sound like her normal self. She sounded like a total zombie. What difference did it make if the coffee cake was eaten at noon on the nose? What if lunch started late—and it was eaten at 12:03, or even 1:03, or even 2:03? Would the cake taste any different? And who eats coffee cake for lunch?

"Well, you'd better eat your pancakes before they get cold!" Mrs. Phonee chirped, scuttling past Penelope before she could ask any more questions. "And say hi to the Chipster for me! I really need to get going. I have lots more cakes to pass around. Cakes don't just deliver themselves, you know...."

The front door slammed behind her.

Well. Penelope had to hand it to Mrs. Phonee: Just when she'd behaved in the weirdest way possible, she always managed to do something even *weirder*.

And weirdest of all, she always got away with it.

CHAPTER FIFTEEN

The Chipster's Homemade Trophy

"Mom?" Penelope asked.

"Yes, dear?" Mom replied cheerily, sipping her coffee.

"Where are Dad and Chip?"

Mom's eyebrows twisted into a puzzled knot. "You know, I'm not quite sure," she said. She paused, her mug of coffee in midair. "I think they mentioned something about the garage. They were going to build something in there...."

"The garage?" Penelope asked, equally as puzzled.

"Yes, your father mentioned something about building a trophy for Chip." All at once Mom straightened, smiling broadly. She slurped from the mug. "Oh, right! I remember now! Your father had just finished making pancakes, and then he and Chip headed to the garage to build a homemade trophy. A trophy in honor of Chip's triumphant victory in the Chip Fritter Pumpkin-Carving Competition at the first annual Chip Fritter Fest! And that's when Mrs. Phonee stopped by. And then . . . hmmm . . . well . . . let's see . . ."

Penelope didn't say a word.

Her eyes narrowed once more.

Now, as you may remember, Penelope's eyes had narrowed many times recently in bafflement and suspicion. But this time, they narrowed to the point where she could barely even *see* out of them. They narrowed to the point where they were barely even teeny little slits.

"What's the matter, sweetheart?" Mom asked.

"I'll tell you what's the matter," Penelope stated gravely. "What's the matter is that a weird woman came to our home. What's the matter is that she asked me— no, *told* me—to baby-sit for her weird kids. What's the matter is that she brought over this weird cake, which she said was only for lunch, but—"

"Hey, guys! It's the Chipster!"

Chip came scrambling into the kitchen.

Dad scrambled after him, carrying—true to Mom's word—a homemade trophy.

"Chip, we were just talking about you!" Mom exclaimed.

"That's so funny," Chip said. "I was just *thinking* about me!"

"What a nice trophy," Mom stated proudly.

Chip shrugged, placing it on the table beside the pancakes.

"It is nice, isn't it? It would have been nicer if the school had given me an actual trophy instead of a medal, but I understand why they didn't. After all, they had their hands full with Chip Fritter Fest. Nobody had *time* to make me a trophy. I don't blame them."

Oh, brother, Penelope thought, rolling her eyes.

"So who's in the mood for some breakfast?" Dad shouted.

"ME!" Mom and Chip shouted together.

"Then let's eat!"

The three of them sat and began wolfing down pancakes.

Penelope stood there, watching. She wanted to ask them a few questions. She wanted to know why nobody really remembered the first annual Chip Fritter Fest.

She wanted to know why Mom had mysteriously decided to take a nap on the table during Mrs. Phonee's visit. She wanted to know a *lot* of things.

But she didn't bother asking.

Instead, she just sat down and began wolfing down pancakes along with the rest of her family.

She *was* hungry, after all.

Besides, chances were that nobody would have listened to her questions anyway.

PART III

The Plot Thickens Even More

CHAPTER SIXTEEN

Vlad Black's Old House

"I really don't know about this," Penelope murmured, staring out the car window as Mom pulled to a stop in front of Vlad Black's old house.

"What's not to know?" Mom asked.

"Vlad Black's old house is sort of spooky," Penelope said. "Isn't it?"

Mom laughed. "But it's not Vlad Black's *old* house anymore, sweetheart! It's the Phonees' *new* house. It's as if Vlad Black never lived there at all!"

Penelope swallowed. Maybe that was true. But

regardless of *who* lived there, it didn't look like the sort of house where she wanted to spend the next three hours baby-sitting two super-tall gray-haired kids. It looked like the sort of house that was haunted, or possessed, or cursed. There was a tower with a rusted weathervane, for Pete's sake. There were darkened stained glass windows and a rickety old porch, too.

"Don't worry, Penelope," Mom soothed. "You're such a wonderful baby-sitter. Just ask the Sips! They thought you were terrific when you baby-sat their kids! We all celebrated your great job afterward, remember?"

"We didn't celebrate my great baby-sitting job, Mom," Penelope muttered. "We celebrated Chip's winning goal in a soccer game."

"Oh, that's right," Mom said. "Well, it was a pretty spectacular goal. The Chipster really came through in the clutch. The chips were down, and—" She broke off and grinned. "Hey, that's a great little catchphrase, isn't it? The 'chips' were down, so 'Chip' really came through in the clutch! Get it? 'Chips' and 'Chip'—"

"I should go, Mom," Penelope mumbled.

"Okay, then. Have fun. Good-bye, Penelope!"

"Good-bye."

Penelope hopped out of the car and slammed the

door behind her, shambling up the front walk. She had to admit it: As much as the notion of baby-sitting two weird, tall, gray-haired kids in a spooky house depressed her, it didn't depress her nearly as much as listening to Mom drone on and on about Chip.

CHAPTER SEVENTEEN

Knock-Knock

Penelope raised the spooky metal knocker and banged it a few times.

A moment later Mrs. Phonee opened up the door.

"Penelope!" she cried, in her oddly familiar, deep voice. She wore lots of makeup, a long purple dress, and big hoop earrings. "Here you are, at eleven o'clock on the nose. You're so prompt! Promptness is the mark of a very responsible baby-sitter."

"Uh, thanks," Penelope said. She stepped inside. She wasn't sure what else she was supposed to say.

Mrs. Phonee swept across the hall toward the staircase and waved her hands in the air. "Mr. Phonee and I need to get ready for our lunch—so please just get started with Boris and Ophelia. They've really been looking forward to today."

Penelope peered around the enormous, shadowy hallway. Unfortunately, Boris and Ophelia were nowhere to be seen.

"Go ahead, Penelope!" Mrs. Phonee cried when she reached the top of the stairs. "Do your baby-sitting thing."

"Um . . . where *are* Boris and Ophelia?" Penelope asked.

"Oh, they're around here somewhere," Mrs. Phonee said. "You know how small kids can be. They're into everything! You might want to try the garage. . . ."

She slammed a door behind her. *Thwack.*

Penelope stood there all by herself. She perked up her ears, listening for the telltale sounds of laughter, or shrieking, or blocks being knocked over—the kind of sounds made by children who were into everything. But the house was dead silent.

That wasn't the real problem, however. The real problem was that Penelope had no idea where the garage was.

CHAPTER EIGHTEEN

Odd Goings-On in the Garage

"Yes, young lady? May I help you?"

Penelope nearly jumped out of her skin. She whirled around.

Mr. Phonee stood right behind her, dressed in a pin-stripe suit and orange tie. He gave her a curious smile.

"Uh . . . hi," she stammered, once she'd managed to collect herself. "I'm—"

"Penelope Fritter!" he interrupted. He smacked his palm against his forehead. "The baby-sitter! Of course! How could I have been so absentminded?" He took her arm and led her out of the hallway. "Follow me. The children are so eager to see you."

Before Penelope had a chance to ask how Mr. Phonee was able to sneak up behind her without making a sound, he steered her down a darkened corridor.

"Boris just loves baby-sitters," Mr. Phonee continued, pushing through a door that opened on a vast three-car garage—a garage almost half the size of the Clearwater Elementary gym. Parked there were a Jeep, a Bug, and a stretch limousine.

A pair of long hairy legs jutted out from under the Jeep.

"Boris?" Mr. Phonee called toward the legs. "The baby-sitter is here."

"The *who*?" growled a voice even deeper than Mrs. Phonee's.

Mr. Phonee grinned apologetically at Penelope, then turned back to the legs. "The baby-sitter, Boris. Remember? Penelope Fritter? Chip Fritter's sister?"

"Chip Fritter's sister!" cried the voice. The legs began to scramble—and an instant later Boris slid out from under the car on a little skateboardlike platform. His clothes and face were covered in grease. He hopped excitedly to his feet. In one hand he held a dirty rag. In the other he held a wrench. "Did she bring the Chipster?"

"No, son, I'm sorry," Mr. Phonee stated in a very

fatherly tone. "I told you earlier that Penelope would be coming alone. The Chipster can't make it today."

Boris stamped his huge feet. "But I want to see the Chipster!" He pouted.

"Bo-ris," Mr. Phonee warned, wagging a finger. "Be polite."

"I'd be polite if the Chipster was here," Boris muttered. He glowered down at Penelope, then dropped back onto the little skateboardlike platform and scooted under the car again.

"I'm sorry about that," whispered Mr. Phonee. He led Penelope back inside the house. "He'll warm up to you once he gets to know you. Let's go say hi to Ophelia. She's puttering around in the kitchen."

Penelope nodded. She was at a loss for words, and not even because Boris had been so rude. No, Penelope was at a loss for words for an entirely different reason: Nothing this family said or did made any sense at all.

Boris was a nine-year-old boy, yet he was hanging out in the garage, fixing his parents' Jeep. He looked right at home there too—as if he were a mechanic. But what sort of nine-year-old worked on his parents' Jeep without his parents' supervision? *Chip* wouldn't even do that, and Chip was fourteen. Chip needed his dad's supervision while making a homemade trophy (a trophy that, to put it nicely, was less than spectacular looking). Penelope could only imagine what Boris would be doing in the garage when he was Chip's age. Building a rocket engine? Performing brain surgery? Talk about a "real superstar" . . . this Boris kid was a *genius*.

"What's the matter, dear?" Mr. Phonee asked as he whisked Penelope toward the kitchen. "You look troubled."

"I was just wondering . . ." Penelope hesitated. "Is Boris *really* nine years old?"

"Oh, yes," Mr. Phonee said, smiling proudly. "You'd be surprised how many people ask that. He's very advanced for his age."

"I guess he is," Penelope agreed. She certainly wasn't going to argue.

CHAPTER NINETEEN

Odder Goings-On in the Kitchen

In the kitchen things were even odder.

Ophelia wasn't merely puttering around. She was *cooking*. And not cooking the way a normal seven-year-old might—pouring a bowl of cereal, making a milk shake, or defrosting frozen waffles.

She was cooking the way a gourmet chef might in a fancy restaurant.

Timers buzzed, pots boiled, and kettles whistled. Everywhere Penelope looked, there were stacks of coffee cakes and piles of Jell-O molds. Ophelia was so busy bustling among all the cakes-in-process and molds-in-the-making that she didn't even notice Mr. Phonee and Penelope standing in the doorway.

"Yoo-hoo!" Mr. Phonee called. "Ophelia, darling, the baby-sitter is here!"

"Who?" Ophelia asked. She withdrew a steaming coffee cake from the oven and placed it into a box, then popped another cake in.

"You remember," Mr. Phonee said. "Penelope? Chip Fritter's sister?"

At the mention of Chip, Ophelia squealed in delight. "Chip Fritter's sister!" She batted her eyelashes and lowered her voice. "Did the Chipster come too?"

"No, Ophelia, Chip isn't here," Mr. Phonee stated. "We discussed this, remember? Penelope will baby-sit you and Boris this afternoon while your mother and I are at lunch."

Ophelia's eyes darkened. "So Chip didn't come?" she asked, as if Penelope wasn't even there.

"No, sweetheart," Mr. Phonee replied.

"Well, fine," she muttered sulkily. "I'm just going to keep cooking, then. And I'd prefer to cook alone."

She ducked down beside the oven again, banging the door closed extra hard.

Mr. Phonee quickly escorted Penelope back to the front hall.

"I'm so sorry," he apologized to Penelope again. "Ophelia just gets a little wound up at this time of day. I'm sure she'll warm up to you once she gets to know you too."

Penelope shrugged. The truth was, she wasn't all that concerned with Ophelia getting to know her. She wasn't so sure if *she* wanted to get to know Ophelia. No, Penelope was a lot more concerned with something else—namely how Ophelia had completely taken over the kitchen, and how Mr. Phonee didn't seem to mind a bit.

Fixing a Jeep was one thing. Maybe Boris was just *pretending* to fix it. The Jeep wasn't running, at least. But Ophelia was cooking up a storm—and it definitely *wasn't* pretend. Not only was the oven running, but the stove was also on, along with the toaster, blender, and mixer. Penelope's mom would never let Penelope take over *their* kitchen like that. And Penelope was five years older than Ophelia.

"What's the matter, Penelope?" Mr. Phonee asked. "You look upset again."

"I'm fine," Penelope mumbled, even though she wasn't. "I was just wondering, though. Is Ophelia really seven?"

"Of course!" Mr. Phonee exclaimed.

"Of course," Penelope repeated. "And let me guess. She's advanced for her age too, right?"

Mr. Phonee burst out laughing. "You don't miss a thing, do you? Just what I like in a baby-sitter!"

Penelope sighed. Too bad she felt as if she'd missed *lots* of things.

She decided to try one final question.

"Um, aren't Ophelia and Boris a little old for naps?" she asked. "I mean, don't most kids stop that sort of thing when they're about three or four?"

Mr. Phonee shrugged. "You've seen how active they are," he said. "Those two are real firecrackers. By noon they'll be totally exhausted."

Penelope nodded slowly. Well, at least that answer made sense. And, on the bright side, she probably wouldn't have to worry about getting Boris and Ophelia ready for their naps. Given how advanced they were, they could probably handle teeth-brushing on their own just fine. She probably wouldn't have to read them a story, either. For all she knew, given how advanced they were, they could not only tuck themselves in, but they had also written their own stories, starring themselves.

CHAPTER TWENTY

The Question Penelope
Wants to Ask Most of All

Mrs. Phonee swept down the staircase to the front hall, her long, purple dress billowing behind her. "Now, just make yourself at home, Penelope," she instructed. "Do your homework, watch TV, anything you like. Boris and Ophelia can take their naps whenever they want. They'll probably just tuck themselves in!"

Penelope stared as Mrs. Phonee looped her arm under Mr. Phonee's and marched toward the front door. "Um . . ."

"Yes, dear?" Mrs. Phonee asked.

"What if there's an emergency?" Penelope asked. "How should I get in touch with you? And what should I do about lunch? Should I let Ophelia prepare it? Do they have any allergies? Are they allowed to watch TV too?"

At first Penelope had planned on asking only one question—but now that she'd opened her mouth, she couldn't seem to close it. And none of the questions she'd just asked even included the one she wanted to ask. No, the one question she *really* wanted to ask, the one that had been nagging at her ever since she'd arrived, was, *Why do I even* need *to baby-sit your two children? They're much more advanced than I am!*

"Oh, how silly of us," Mr. Phonee said. He exchanged a quick frown with Mrs. Phonee, then dug into his pocket and pulled out a business card. "Here is my cell phone number. If there are any problems, feel free to call us." He stared at Penelope. "But I'm sure there won't be any problems, will there?"

Penelope gulped. Mr. Phonee didn't sound as if he were *asking* her if there would be any problems. He sounded as if he were *telling* her that there *shouldn't* be any problems. He sounded as if he were giving her an order.

"No, sir," Penelope heard herself reply.

"Good," he said, smiling again.

"And as far as lunch goes," Mrs. Phonee added, "Ophelia and Boris usually just snack on Ophelia's coffee cakes and Jell-O molds all day. They can skip lunch and go right into naptime if they like."

Penelope shook her head, utterly bewildered.

In all her life, she'd never, *ever* heard of two parents allowing their kids to skip a meal and go straight to sleep. (Especially if those kids had been eating cake and Jell-O molds all day.) Skipping a meal and going straight to bed was usually a *punishment*. Penelope was almost tempted to tell Mr. and Mrs. Phonee that she would be happy to make Boris and Ophelia a healthy salad, or a bowl of soup, or even a sandwich. But by the time she decided to speak up, Mr. and Mrs. Phonee had already slammed the front door behind them.

SMACK!

PART IV

Big, Big Trouble

CHAPTER TWENTY-ONE

Not Much Else to Do

For a while Penelope wandered around the big spooky house by herself.

She didn't really have much else to do. She'd brought along her homework as well as a few word scramble books, but she didn't even bother to unzip her backpack. She knew she'd never be able to concentrate; the house was just way too creepy.

And she certainly didn't need to work very hard at baby-sitting. Boris was still in the garage, busily working away on the Jeep. Ophelia was still in the kitchen, busily cooking up coffee cakes and Jell-O molds. It was very clear that neither wanted her company. And a funny thing happened (not "ha-ha" funny, either): The more Penelope wandered around, the more she realized that the house was just as odd as the family who lived in it.

It wasn't *spooky*, exactly—at least, not as spooky as it was on the outside. But certain things were just a little . . . off. For starters, the floors and walls were coated in dust. Many of the lightbulbs were burned out. Lots of furniture was damaged or worn.

In other words, it didn't look like a house that had been recently moved into. It looked like a house that had been lived in by the same people for a very, very long time—people who didn't take very good care of it.

But that wasn't the oddest part of all. The oddest part was that many pictures of Vlad Black still hung on the walls. Wouldn't the Phonee family want to take those down? Pictures weren't like sweatshirts, after all. Pictures didn't keep people warm. They didn't really serve any useful purpose, especially pictures of a not-so-evil villain.

But Penelope decided not to worry about it.

Nope. She had another two-and some-odd hours left here, and she needed something to take her mind off the oddness of it all. And whatever that something was,

it had to be easier than homework or word scrambles.

Fortunately, on the second floor she stumbled on a tiny room with a huge television. She sank into a dusty armchair and flicked on the remote.

Maybe I'll just hang out here until Mr. and Mrs. Phonee get home, Penelope thought to herself. *Watching TV will kill some time.* Unfortunately, the TV didn't get very many channels. The Phonees didn't subscribe to cable. More unfortunate than that, the only programs on at this hour were local news broadcasts—and all of them seemed to be running features on yesterday's Chip Fritter Fest.

"Here we are at the home of the superstar himself," one anchorman announced. "The Chipster really—"

Click. Penelope switched the channel.

"CHIP CHIP HOORAY for—"

Click. Penelope switched the channel again.

"When the Chips are down, the Chipster—"

CLACK!

Penelope turned the TV off for good. For a moment she sat there, scowling. Then she pushed herself out of the dusty chair and marched downstairs. She figured she might as well check up on Ophelia and Boris. It wasn't as if she had anything else to do.

CHAPTER TWENTY-TWO

A Horribly Grim Moment of Panic

"Ophelia?" Penelope called, strolling into the kitchen. "I was just—"

She lurched to a sudden stop. *Uh-oh.* Ophelia was gone. Stranger than that, the entire kitchen had been cleaned. It was spotless. The coffee cakes had vanished; the Jell-O molds had disappeared; the appliances had all been turned off. Strangest of all, the back door was wide open, flapping in the autumn wind.

"Ophelia?" Penelope called again, a little louder this time.

There was no answer.

Penelope's heart thumped. She poked her head out the back door.

"OPHELIA!" she hollered into the yard.

But Ophelia didn't answer. No one did. All Penelope heard were birds chirping.

As fast as she could, Penelope ducked back inside and raced to the garage. "Boris?" she called. "Boris, do you know where your sister—"

She froze.

The color drained from her face.

Boris was no longer in the garage. Neither was the Jeep he'd been working on.

CHAPTER TWENTY-THREE

Events Turn Weirder, but with a Hopeful Upside

Now, if you remember Penelope's previous adventure with the Sip children, you might remember that she did not normally talk to herself out loud. But seeing as these circumstances weren't normal—that they were particularly grim and horrible, and that she was in big, big trouble—she couldn't quite help it.

"Okay," she whispered. "I am not going to panic. Both Mr. and Mrs. Phonee said I was a responsible baby-sitter, and that's exactly what I'm going to be. I am going to find Boris and Ophelia, just like I found the two very awful Sip brats when *they* disappeared. I'm going to find Boris and Ophelia if it's the last thing I do."

With that, Penelope strode back to the kitchen.

Maybe Ophelia left me a note, she thought. It was certainly a possibility, given how "advanced" Ophelia was. *Anything* was a possibility, given this family.

Penelope scoured the shiny counters and cupboards, the glossy refrigerator and freezer doors, looking for a scrap of paper or a Post-it. But she didn't find one.

What she did find, however, were two small burlap sacks, tucked behind the garbage can.

One sack was labeled TXEAR TNGRSEHT LNPESIGE DPROEW.

The other was labeled ERTAX SHRTNGTE EMINASA WRPOED.

"Great," Penelope breathed miserably to herself. "Not only have the weird, overgrown, gray-haired Phonee children disappeared, but now it looks like the Phonee family label their items in some sort of freakish secret language that's total gibberish."

But just as she was saying these words to herself out loud, a thought occurred to her. Those words didn't look like *gibberish*. Well, they did—but more to the point, they looked like the kind of words Penelope would find in one of her word scramble books.

So maybe that was what they were: word scrambles.

CHAPTER TWENTY-FOUR

The Puzzle Comes Together, and Not in a Good Way

Penelope grabbed a pen off the counter. She was about to start working, when suddenly she hesitated. Usually she loved a good word scramble, of course. But she recalled doing a word scramble when she baby-sat the very awful Sip brats too. And it got her into a lot of trouble. She learned way too much about the Sips' disgusting smoothie ingredients and wound up never being able to eat anything strawberry again.

Penelope shook her head. Given how grim and horrible the circumstances were, she really didn't have much of a choice. Unscrambling the letters and cracking the code might offer some clues about Ophelia and Boris's whereabouts—and that was all that mattered. She uncapped the pen and got to work.

A minute passed.... Then two ... then three ...

Penelope's mind raced feverishly as she crossed out the letters and rearranged them. And suddenly both solutions struck her. They struck her as powerfully as the spanking she wanted to give Boris and Ophelia for running away....

(If you'd like to unscramble the words yourself, go right ahead. Penelope's answers are at the bottom of this page.)

TXEAR TNGRSEHT LNPESIGE DPROEW: _____

ERTAX SHRTNGTE EMINASA WRPOED: _____

Penelope stared at the solutions. She stared for a very long time—longer than three minutes, even. She wished she could feel happy at solving the word scrambles. But she couldn't. She felt horrified. Yes, she knew that there was something odd about the Phonees, but *this*? What did these word scrambles even *mean*?

Exhausted, Penelope flopped down at the kitchen table and struggled to figure out was going on. But she couldn't. Her mind kept drawing blanks—

SOLUTION TO SACK #1: EXTRA STRENGTH SLEEPING POWDER

SOLUTION TO SACK #2: EXTRA STRENGTH AMNESIA POWDER

"That's IT!" she suddenly cried.

Her voice was so loud that it echoed off the spooky walls, but Penelope couldn't have cared less. Not only had she solved the scrambles, but she'd also solved the whole *puzzle*. (Or part of it, anyway—and definitely an important part.) And all of the clues pointed to her memory lapse:

• When the Phonees first appeared at the Chip Fritter Fest, they'd insisted that everyone eat their orange turkey-shaped Jell-O mold.

• After Penelope had taken a bite, she couldn't remember a thing.

• When she *could* start remembering, she found herself in the car, as if she'd just woken up from a nap.

• *Plus*, nobody else in her family could remember a thing either.

• So . . .

Mrs. Phonee must have sprinkled these two powders into her Jell-O mold. The sleeping powder made everyone fall asleep at the gym, and the amnesia powder made everyone *forget* that they fell asleep. And now that Penelope really thought about it, Mrs. Phonee probably even sprinkled some sleeping powder and amnesia powder into Mom's coffee yesterday morning, which was why Mom took a nap on the kitchen table and couldn't remember a thing—

Penelope's heart squeezed.

Oh, no.

Mrs. Phonee had brought over that coffee cake, too. And she'd insisted that the Fritters eat it at twelve o'clock on the nose. And Ophelia had been *making* coffee cakes. She'd been making Jell-O molds, too—lots of both. And now all the coffee cakes and Jell-O molds had been cleared out of the kitchen. *And* the Jeep was missing. *And* Mrs. Phonee had told Penelope's mom that she'd needed to deliver her coffee cakes all over town.

Penelope glanced up at the kitchen clock.

It was twelve o'clock. On the nose.

So if Mrs. Phonee had succeeded in passing all her coffee cakes around, and if every single person in Clearwater had eaten a piece of cake when instructed, then the entire town would be asleep. And they wouldn't remember it. Which meant the Phonees . . .

Well, it meant the Phonees could do whatever they wanted.

And judging from what Penelope knew of them so far, she wagered that they wouldn't want to do something good.

CHAPTER TWENTY-FIVE

Penelope Makes a Very Tough Decision

Penelope jumped up and grabbed the telephone.

First she dialed the Phonees' cell number.

It didn't work. The call didn't even connect. The number wasn't in service.

"I should have known," she muttered. Next she tried the police station. But there was no answer. The phone there just rang and rang and rang.

So she tried the fire department. No luck there, either.

Finally, she tried her own home. Still nothing—the

answering machine picked up. "Hi, you've reached the Fritter residence, home of the Chipster!" Chip's recorded voice replied. "To leave a message for me, press one. To leave a message for anyone else, please wait for the tone."

BEEP!

"Mom! Dad! Chip! Wake up!" Penelope cried into the mouthpiece. "Please! Don't eat the coffee cake!" But there was no response. She knew it was too late. Everybody must have already eaten the coffee cake.

Penelope's breath started coming fast. Her heart galloped like a thoroughbred horse. *Don't panic!* she yelled silently at herself. She knew she had to stop the Phonees, whatever they were doing. At the very least, she had to find Boris and Ophelia. It was up to her and her alone. But how? She was just one person. A small person. Boris and Ophelia were very tall. Plus, they seemed to have taken the family Jeep. How could Penelope catch up with them, let alone *find* them? It wasn't like she was a superhero. . . .

Okay. Well. Yes. Right . . . technically, she *was* a superhero, but as far as Penelope was concerned, she was a totally *lame* superhero. And besides, she'd sworn she'd never use her superpowers again. She'd even given up eating anything strawberry, which, as you probably remember, was her favorite flavor.

On the other hand, this *was* an extreme emergency. The entire town was asleep. Using her Super-Sitter powers against the Phonees was the only possible way that she could *stop* the Phonees.

Penelope eyed the refrigerator. She could hear the kitchen clock ticking. It was very loud, in fact. And very annoying.

She did miss eating strawberries—a lot. And if eating strawberries was the only possible way she could trigger her superpowers . . .

"Whatever," she groaned. With a long sigh, she sauntered over to the refrigerator and began rifling through it. *Hmm.* Now that she'd made up her mind, her mouth had started watering. She really needed a strawberry, and she needed it *now.* The problem was that the Phonees' fridge seemed to house every type of berry flavoring except strawberry. There was a jar of raspberry jam, a dish of cranberry sauce, a bottle of blueberry syrup, but nothing strawberry. . . .

"Aha!" Penelope cried.

In the very bottom drawer, tucked behind various cake ingredients, was a tiny dish of strawberry Jell-O, covered with a single sheet of plastic wrap.

CHAPTER TWENTY-SIX

A Stomachache on the Outside

Penelope gobbled down the Jell-O as quickly as she could.

To be fair, she didn't even really gobble it, as the word "gobble" implies chewing. Penelope simply tilted the dish and poured the entire serving of strawberry Jell-O right down her throat. And until she did, she hadn't even realized how much she missed strawberry. It was the coolest, most refreshing, most wonderfully delicious Jell-O she had ever tasted in her life.

"Ahhh," she said, smacking her lips. She slipped the

little dish into the dishwasher. And as she did, she noticed a familiar feeling. *Very* familiar. Or rather . . . it was a familiar pain. Her stomach began to hurt. Only it didn't hurt on the inside—as one might expect it would after she'd slurped down a bowl of strange Jell-O in one gulp. It hurt on the outside.

Penelope glanced down.

And there it was! That thick black belt! It had magically appeared, tied around her waist. And tied too tightly, which was why it hurt. Penelope had hoped she'd never see that belt and its pouches full of weird baby items again. But now she couldn't help but breathe a sigh of relief. This weird belt and its weird items were her only hope. And everything looked just as she remembered.

The first pouch held a small bottle labeled SUPER STICKY BABY POWDER.

The second pouch held a clothespin labeled SUPER CLOTHESPIN OF TRUTH.

The third pouch held a diaper dispenser labeled SUPER ABSORBANT DIAPERS. A diaper pin also stuck out from this pouch. It was labeled SUPER STRONG DIAPER PIN.

And the fourth pouch held a teeny-weeny little black book—a black book that Penelope remembered *very* well.

CHAPTER TWENTY-SEVEN

The Teeny-Weeny Little Black Book

Penelope yanked the book out of its pouch and tore it open to the first page.

Congratulations! It's been a while! We're proud that you've made the decision to eat strawberry. You remembered the rule: STRAWBERRY = SUPERPOWERS.

Now that you're a superhero again, you have the honor of being back in league with the likes of Bad Breath Billy, Ms. Leapfrog, Charlie Chores, and

Round Round Robin, also known as Super Bouncy Girl and occasionally referred to as What's-Her-Face in some parts of the United States and Canada.

Penelope frowned. This wasn't any help at all. She decided to skip ahead to the next page.

In case you don't remember, your amazing super-powers last for only one hour at a time, so you really need to act quickly. If we were you, we'd climb the tallest tree you can find and see if you can spot the Phonees from there. Otherwise you'll be in big, big trouble!

Penelope didn't waste another second. As irritating as this teeny-weeny little black book was, it had never steered her wrong in the past. She shoved it back into its pouch and then bolted out of the house.

PART V

The Extraordinarily
Surprising Conclusion

CHAPTER TWENTY-EIGHT

The Getaway Jeep

Penelope darted first to her left, then to her right. She ran up and down the street, desperately searching for a very tall tree.

But there *were* no tall trees on the block where the Phonees lived—only squat little shrubs. There were a few very tall streetlamps, however.

Finally Penelope stood below the lamppost directly in front of the Phonees' house. She gasped for air, scowling up at the bulb. *Hmm*, she thought. *If that teeny-weeny little black book is so smart, why didn't it mention streetlamps?*

But there was no point in asking any questions she couldn't answer. She knew she had to make do with what she had. So she removed the bottle labeled SUPER STICKY BABY POWDER from the pouch.

She sprinkled some dust on her hands.

It burst from the bottle in a puffy cloud: *Pfffft!!*

The very next instant she could feel it beginning to grow sticky. Her palms started getting all gooey and tingly and tight, as if they were covered with lots of melted candy. She was ready. There was no time to waste.

Penelope jumped onto the lamppost and shimmied up as fast as she could.

"Wow," she whispered to herself. The Super Sticky Baby Powder was even sticker than she remembered. She felt as if she were a human fly. Well, either that or a human magnet. In fact, she wondered if she would be able to *un*stick herself. The powder was pretty strong. . . .

By the time she reached the very top of the lamppost—the part where the light jutted out over the street on a narrow metal arch—she had to use all her might to yank her sticky hands off the cold metal.

For a very scary few seconds, she wobbled on top of the little arch.

Yikes.

From where she sat, the ground looked very far away. It looked much farther away than the top of the lamppost had looked from the ground, actually. But at least she could see the entire town of Clearwater from this frighteningly narrow perch. She could see all the way to her house. She could also see her school, and Chip's school, and—

The Phonees' Jeep!

CHAPTER TWENTY-NINE

Not Very Much Help

Yes, there it was: the Phonees' Jeep, screeching down a narrow side street a few blocks away!

Penelope was certain it was the Phonees' Jeep too. No doubt about it. Because the driver's side window was open, and Boris was sitting there at the wheel, his dumb plastic propeller hat spinning in the wind. Penelope squinted, straining her eyes to see more closely. Boris wasn't alone, either . . . someone was sitting beside him, someone with lots of boxes in her lap, the sorts of boxes you might pack a coffee cake in. . . .

"Ophelia!" Penelope cried.

She nearly fell off the lamppost.

Okay, she said to herself. *Okay. Like I said before, fixing a car is one thing. But* driving *a car? No nine-year-old drives a car. Something is definitely wrong here.*

A lot of things were wrong, of course.

Mainly, though, the *most* wrong thing was that she had to chase that Jeep, and it was getting away—and she was stuck atop a lamppost. Even with the help of her Super Sticky Baby Powder, it would still take time to climb down to the street.

Penelope glanced down at her thick black belt. Her gaze came to rest on the Super Absorbent Diapers. A thought prickled in her brain. If these diapers were as strong as the Super Sticky Baby Powder, maybe she could fashion a little lasso out of them and swing from lamppost to lamppost over to the Jeep.

Actually, on second thought, that might be a little dangerous.

Actually, on third thought, that might just be down-right stupid.

Then again, so was scaling a lamppost and sitting on top of it.

Penelope's eyes flashed over to the teeny-weeny little black book. She tore it open to page three.

We haven't the faintest clue how to help you here. You climbed a lamppost. We recommended that you climb a tree. If you'd looked a little harder, you might have found a tree. Besides, we may be superintelligent aliens, but you're the superhero. Oh—and not to be irritating—but you're also running out of time.

All the best,

The Super-Intelligent Aliens

CHAPTER THIRTY

A Stupid Idea
Is Made *Un*stupid

"Thanks for nothing," muttered Penelope. So it looked as if she didn't have much of a choice. She could trust her own first idea—which might be a little dangerous, if not downright stupid—or she could keep sitting here on top of the lamppost while Boris and Ophelia got away.

And right then, she made up her mind. *No way* was she going to let Boris and Ophelia get away.

Penelope yanked a diaper from the dispenser. Then she yanked out another, and another . . . and, fingers flying, she began roping them all together into a makeshift lasso. She sealed the knots with diaper tape. In less than two minutes, the lasso was nearly as long as the lamppost itself.

Then she hopped to her feet.

Yikes, she thought again, teetering.

But she ignored the terrible depths below her. She ignored how much her limbs were wobbling. She ignored how narrow and fragile the little metal arch was. . . .

Instead she swung the lasso around her head several times, cowboy-style—faster and faster. When it was whirling so fast that she couldn't even see it, she let it fly. *Whoooosh!!!*

In a blur it shot toward the next lamppost and hooked around the lightbulb.

Penelope closed her eyes and leaped off the metal arch, clinging to her lasso with her super-sticky hands. She fell freely and gracefully through the air, until—

Thud!!!

"Oof," Penelope groaned.

Her nose had smacked right into a cold metal pole. She winced, opening her eyes. Her idea *was* stupid, she realized. She was now dangling from another lamppost, and Boris and Ophelia were speeding away in their Jeep. But that was okay, because she also realized something else. She realized exactly how to make her idea *un*stupid.

She shouldn't swing to the *next* lamppost. She should skip the next lamppost—the lamppost to which she'd tied her super-strong diaper lasso—and then swing to the lamppost *beyond*. And then she should repeat the process.

That way, she'd practically *fly* over town.

CHAPTER THIRTY-ONE

The Plan Works (The Plan to Fly Over Town, That Is)

And that's precisely what Penelope did.

She swung through the air—using one lamppost as a swing, and the next as a landing pad, whirling her lasso as fast as she could. . . .

Gradually drawing closer and closer to the Phonees' Jeep . . .

Until finally, the Phonees' Jeep screeched to a stop, right outside the Clearwater town bank . . .

. . . and Penelope swung down, right in front of them!

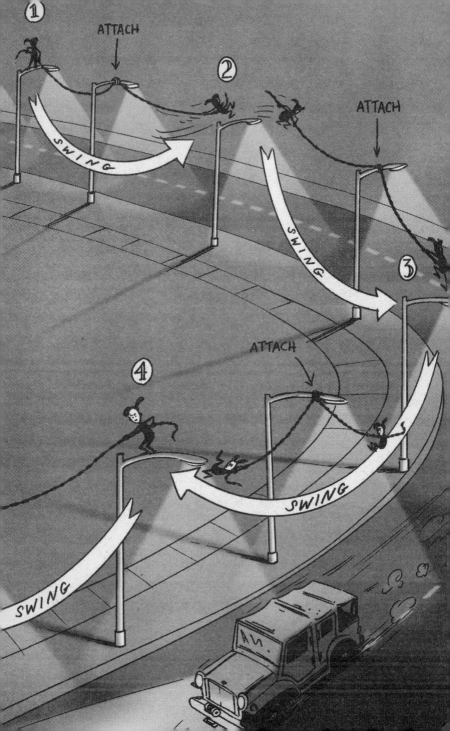

CHAPTER THIRTY-TWO

The Suspenseful Showdown

"Stop it right there!" Penelope shouted, raising a hand.

Boris and Ophelia gaped at her through the windshield.

"What are *you* doing here?" Boris demanded.

"Yeah," Ophelia chimed in. "Aren't you supposed to be doing your homework?"

Penelope folded her arms across her chest. "The question you should be asking is, what are *you* doing here?" she replied.

(As soon as she'd asked that question, though,

Penelope felt a little silly. After all, *they* would never ask what *they* were doing here. They knew very well what they were doing here.)

Boris and Ophelia exchanged a smirk.

Penelope glowered at them. She began spinning her diaper lasso, faster and faster. She'd had just about enough of these weird, tall, gray-haired, overgrown "advanced" kids. She was going to rope them up and drag them down to the police station, and sit there all night if she had to, until everyone woke up—

"Penelope?" a deep, familiar voice asked.

Penelope spun around.

Mrs. Phonee stood in front of the bank, alongside Mr. Phonee, staring angrily at her. Both were dragging huge bags behind them. On each bag was printed the same symbol.

Penelope understood the symbol immediately. It didn't need to be unscrambled.

It was the classic symbol found on bags used by all villains who robbed banks.

The label read $$$.

CHAPTER THIRTY-THREE

The REALLY
Suspenseful Showdown

"What are YOU doing here?" Mrs. Phonee demanded. "You should be at our house, doing your homework!"

"Or watching TV!" Mr. Phonee added crossly.

Penelope rolled her eyes. "I thought I was supposed to be baby-sitting your kids," she said. "But it looks like I didn't have to, eh?"

Mrs. Phonee squinted at her. "Did you just say 'eh'? Who says 'eh'? Who do you think you are, anyway? Some kind of superhero?"

Mr. Phonee smacked Mrs. Phonee's arm. "Who *cares* what she said? Let's just get out of here! NOW!"

Penelope tried to open her mouth once more for another witty remark. But before she could, Mr. and Mrs. Phonee had barreled straight past her and into the Jeep.

"DRIVE!" Mr. and Mrs. Phonee screamed at once.

Boris gunned the engine.

The tires squealed in a hiss of smoke as he tore down the street.

Penelope felt a surge of anger. She felt a surge of righteous, superhero indignation! How dare they try to escape! She shot a quick peek inside the open bank door. Every single teller and security guard was snoozing amidst boxes of empty coffee cakes. So. It was up to her, and her alone, to stop these villains.

Once again she began to twirl her diaper lasso.

And at the exact instant that Boris was about to round the corner onto the next block, she let the diaper lasso fly: *Whoooosh!* It shot through the air and wrapped around the Jeep's tailpipe: *Phhht!* And in the same miraculous and skillful move, Penelope used her other hand to sprinkle some Super Sticky Baby Powder onto the pavement. She planted her feet squarely in the middle of the pile: *Stomp!*

Now she couldn't move.

And neither could the Phonees.

"Ha!" Penelope laughed. No matter how hard Boris pressed on the gas pedal, the Jeep was still stuck. She allowed herself another little smile.

Then she realized something.

She was stuck too. Her feet were glued to the pavement. So she wasn't going anywhere either.

Oh, brother, she thought. She reached into the big black belt and pulled out the teeny-weeny little black book, flipping it open to page four.

> *Great idea using the diapers as a lasso! We thought you were a goner!*
>
> *You still might be a goner, actually. Your hour is almost up.*
> *All the best,*
> *The Super-Intelligent Aliens*

Penelope slammed the book shut.

Nice. She really should have known better. It was now abundantly clear to her that the teeny-weeny little black book would *never* help her unless she helped herself. She shoved it back into its pouch . . . then hesitated.

She'd caught a glimpse of the Super Safety Pin.

CHAPTER THIRTY-FOUR

The Most Brilliant Idea
of the Entire Day

Penelope wasn't even *aware* that she was having the most brilliant idea of the entire day. Her brain was moving too fast. She grabbed the Super Safety Pin from the thick black belt and jammed it through her end of the diaper lasso—then, summoning all her strength, she plunged it down into the street.

It stuck.

Not only did it stick, it couldn't even *move*, even if Penelope had wanted to move it.

Penelope laughed again: "Ha!" Because sticking the Super Safety Pin into the street wasn't even the most brilliant part of her brilliant plan. No, the most brilliant part was also, by far, the easiest:

She wriggled out of her shoes.

You see, her *shoes* were stuck to the pavement with Super Sticky Diaper Powder. Not her feet. Her feet were free to roam wherever she chose—which was straight toward the Phonees' Jeep.

She padded right up to the back door in her stocking feet and flung it open.

"You!" she shouted at Mrs. Phonee, who stared back at her in open-mouthed rage. "Tell me who you are!"

Mrs. Phonee snickered. "Why should I?"

Penelope blinked. That was actually a very good question. Mrs. Phonee and her freakish family had not only robbed a bank, but they'd dosed the entire town with sleeping *and* amnesia powders. So it didn't seem very likely that Mrs. Phonee would be big on telling the truth. Especially when it concerned revealing her true identity.

But Penelope had an easy solution for that problem.

She reached into her thick black belt and removed the Super Clothespin of Truth. Then she reached over and snapped it right onto the end of Mrs. Phonee's ugly, heavily made-up nose.

CHAPTER THIRTY-FIVE

Mrs. Phonee Confesses, Thanks to the Clothespin

"So who are you?" Penelope demanded again.

"Vlad Black," Mrs. Phonee answered.

Penelope burst out laughing. She couldn't help it. Of all the outrageous lies Mrs. Phonee had told . . .

But then she stopped laughing. A little shiver ran down her spine.

Wait a second—

"I'm wearing a wig, a dress, and some makeup," Mrs. Phonee said. "See?"

She grabbed her hair and yanked it off in one fell swoop.

Penelope's jaw dropped. It *was* Vlad Black! No wonder that voice had sounded so familiar! No wonder those black eyes had looked so evil! (Okay . . . actually, those black eyes had never really looked evil at all, but they certainly looked evil now. Or maybe not so much evil as tired.)

"Bu—but you skipped town, right after I caught you trying to steal the Sips' secret smoothie recipe!" Penelope stammered.

Vlad Black nodded. "Right," he said. His deep voice sounded nasal and silly, thanks to the Super Clothespin of Truth. "And when I left town, I tried to figure out the formula all by myself. But I accidentally invented super sleeping powder and super amnesia powder instead. So I enlisted the help of three other evil masterminds. Well, actually I just enlisted the help of my cousins, Boris, Ophelia, and Sheldon here, who's posing as Mr. Phonee."

"Sheldon?" Penelope asked.

Mr. Phonee shrugged. "That's my name."

"Maybe they aren't quite masterminds," Vlad Black continued, "but they are pretty evil. Or at least they're the most evil people I know. Although they're really pretty nice if you get to know them . . . anyway, speaking of evil, our plan was to return to town posing as the Phonee family—then put the whole town to sleep with our evil baked goods and search for the Sips' recipe. But we realized that with the whole town asleep, we could do a lot more than just look for a smoothie recipe! We could rob a bank!"

Penelope grimaced.

"What?" Vlad Black asked.

"That's the most awful thing I've ever heard," Penelope mumbled. "That *is* evil."

Vlad cackled wickedly, the Super Clothespin of Truth shimmying on top of his nose. "I know! That was the beauty of it! There was only one problem: You! You were already on to me in the first place. So I knew that no matter how well the powders worked, I had to keep you occupied with a phony baby-sitting job."

Penelope shook her head. "So Boris and Ophelia *aren't* nine and seven," she murmured, mostly to herself.

"Please, honey." Ophelia chuckled. "I'm old enough to be your grandma."

CHAPTER THIRTY-SIX

No More Questions,
No More Answers

All at once a deafening clang filled the air.

GONG.

Penelope glanced up. The clock tower on top of the bank had struck one o'clock. Suddenly her stomach felt much better. She glanced down.

Her thick black belt had disappeared.

Uh-oh, she thought.

Her thick black belt wasn't the only thing that had disappeared. To Penelope's horror, the diaper lasso was gone too—along with the Super Strong Diaper Pin jammed into the pavement and the Super Clothespin of Truth clipped to Vlad Black's nose.

Penelope blinked at Vlad Black.

Vlad Black blinked back.

But before either of them had a chance to run, or chase, or scream, several guards stumbled out of the bank door. They groggily rubbed their eyes. Several police officers also pulled up behind the Jeep in their police cars. They yawned sleepily. The police chief looked sleepiest of all.

"What's going on here?" the police chief croaked. His voice was still hoarse from his nap.

Penelope didn't answer. Luckily, neither did Vlad Black nor his gang—though probably for different reasons. Penelope didn't answer because she had no answer. What could she possibly say? That Vlad Black had tricked the whole town, dressed as a woman, with a fake husband and two fake gray-haired children? That she'd foiled his evil plot with her strawberry-induced superpowers?

And as these questions occurred to her, a sleepy crowd began to gather. The whole town was waking up at the same time. And from the middle of the crowd, much to Penelope's utter surprise, her entire family emerged— yawning and rubbing their eyes, like all the rest.

"Mom? Dad? Chip?" Penelope asked. "What are you guys doing here?"

"Chip thought it would be nice if you had some company baby-sitting today," Mom said. "So we started to walk over to the Phonees . . . and then . . ."

"We had some coffee cake on the way over," Dad added. "Seeing as it was twelve o'clock and all . . ."

"And we woke up in the middle of a ditch!" Chip concluded cheerfully.

Penelope frowned.

"Miss?" the police chief asked Penelope. "You didn't answer my question. What's going on? Who are these people in this Jeep?"

"These people are THIEVES!" Penelope shrieked. "Look at their bags!" She jerked a finger at the big $$$ symbols.

The police chief peered into the backseat.

Then he turned to Chip. "Chip?" he asked. "Did you capture these thieves?"

Chip shrugged. "Honestly, I can't remember. I ate some cake, then woke up in a ditch . . . and, well, here I am!"

"Well actually, I—" Penelope said, taking a step forward.

"I think you captured them, Chipster!" shouted somebody from the crowd.

"Me too!" shouted somebody else.

"But I really—" stammered Penelope.

"Me three!" shouted a third.

Penelope shook her head. This was hopeless.

"You know," said Chip, thinking for a minute. "It does sound like something I'd do, doesn't it?"

"Of course it does, sweetie!" Mrs. Fritter cried.

"You're a real superstar!" Mr. Fritter agreed.

The police chief nodded somberly as Vlad Black and his gang were arrested. "Well, it's apparent to me that nobody else but Chip could have captured these villains," he said. "Once again, the town of Clearwater owes the Chipster a debt of gratitude."

Vlad Black and his gang poked their heads out of the nearby police wagon and shouted, "Is there anything Chip Fritter can't do?"

"CHIP CHIP HOORAY!" roared the crowd.

The villains waved a tearful good-bye to Chip as the wagon rolled away.

Penelope sighed. It certainly hadn't taken long for things in Clearwater to get back to normal.

CHAPTER THIRTY-SEVEN

What EVER Will I Feed Them?

Penelope padded over to her shoes, which she'd abandoned during the superhero incident. When she was done tying them, she walked over to the Phonee's Jeep and peeked inside. Ophelia's desserts were still piled high in the passenger seat.

"There you are!" Mrs. Fritter cried, running up to Penelope. "We're all heading back to the house to celebrate Chip's heroic act! I knew you wouldn't want to miss it!"

"Uh, great," Penelope said, forcing herself to smile.

"I invited anyone who wanted to celebrate with Chip," Mrs. Fritter explained, her face clouding over with worry. "So of course *everyone* wants to come. And now I just don't know what I'll feed them all. . . ."

Penelope shook her head. She had no solution. Suddenly she remembered Ophelia's coffee cakes and Jell-O molds. But no, no . . . she couldn't. No way. No matter how annoying it would be to have the whole town in her home shouting, "CHIP CHIP HOORAY," she could never, ever suggest that her mother serve tainted—

"What are all these?" Mrs. Fritter asked, as she opened the door to Boris's Jeep. She began poking around Ophelia's dessert boxes.

"Oh, those belonged to Vlad Black," Penelope explained. "But you really can't take them because they're—"

"Well, I know they're evidence, dear," Mrs. Fritter said. "But they *are* just pastries. And Chip *is* the one who captured the criminals. I'm going to ask the police officers if I can take a few. The entire force is coming to the celebration, so I'm sure they'll want something to eat. . . ."

Penelope rolled her eyes. Things really *were* back to normal in Clearwater. She was invisible again.

But on the plus side, if her mother served Ophelia's desserts at the celebration, she wouldn't have to listen to everyone shouting, "CHIP CHIP HOORAY." They'd be too busy snoring.

Sometimes being invisible wasn't such a bad thing.

Yes, Penelope had to admit: Sometimes being invisible had its sunny side.

THE END

Questions for Next Time:

1. Will Vlad Black and his evil gang return?

2. Will Mrs. Fritter serve tainted pastries at her Chip Fritter celebration?

3. Will Penelope meet the other superheroes mentioned in the teeny-weeny little black book? **Finally?** (If you remember, this was also question number two from last time.)

4. Will the town of Clearwater learn that Chip Fritter was, in fact, **not** responsible for the apprehension of Vlad Black and his evil gang?

5. Will Penelope ever eat strawberry again?

6. Will Clearwater Elementary hold another Chip Fritter Fest?

7. Do you find the super-intelligent aliens as irritating as Penelope does?

For the answers to all these questions and more, please tune in to the next exciting installment of . . .

PENELOPE FRITTER: SUPER-SITTER!*

*Answers will most certainly not be included in next installment.